Mystery
of the
Ballerina
Ghost

Carson –

enjoy the journey!

Janelle + lisa

Mystery
of the
Ballerina
Ghost

BY JANELLE DILLER
ILLUSTRATIONS BY ADAM TURNER

Published by WorldTrek Publishing

Copyright © 2013 by Pack-n-Go Girls

Printed in the USA

Visit our website at www.packngogirls.com.

This is a work of fiction. Names, characters, places, and incidents either are the product of the author's imagination or are used fictitiously. The town of Kitzbühel, Austria, is real, and it's a wonderful place to visit. Any other resemblance to actual events, locales, organizations, or persons, living or dead, is entirely coincidental and beyond the intent of either the author or the publisher.

Illustrations by Adam Turner

ISBN 978-1-936376-00-1

Cataloging-in-Publication Data available from the Library of Congress.

In memory of my dad, who taught me to love the adventure of the journey as much as the pleasure of the destination.

Contents

Meet the Characters

Brooke Mason is crazy about horses! She can't wait to see the castle they'll be staying in.

Eva Mueller is lighter than air when she dances. She's really excited to show Brooke the castle.

Mrs. Mason is Brooke's mom. She loves art more than anything—except her family, of course.

Herr Mueller is Eva's grandfather. He's the master of the castle, Schloss Mueller.

The Ballerina Ghost
isn't giving up her secrets!

And now, the mystery begins . . .

Mystery of the Ballerina Ghost

Chapter One

Austria! (Not Australia!)

Brooke Mason plopped down on her suitcase. She was Tired.

Brooke knew only proper nouns should be capitalized in the middle of a sentence. She also knew "tired" wasn't a proper noun. But she was tired enough to make it a capital letter anyway. Mrs. Harvey, her third grade teacher from last year, would just have to understand.

The clock on the airport wall said 10:42.

That made it 10:42 in the morning in Austria. Brooke's watch said 2:42. That made it 2:42 in the middle of the night in Colorado. She should be sound asleep in her own bed, not dragging her suitcase through an airport. She hadn't even stayed up this late at the last slumber party she went to. In fact, Brooke wasn't sure she'd Ever stayed up this late.

In this case, "ever" deserved a capital letter, too.

Brooke tugged at her mom's sleeve. "So when will we get to see kangaroos?"

"Huh?" Mrs. Mason's eyes were only half open. It was 2:42 in the middle of the night for her, too.

"All my friends told me to make sure I send them pictures of kangaroos. Isn't that what Australia is famous for?"

Mrs. Mason's eyes opened a tiny bit wider. "Honey, we're in Austria, *not* Australia. We're in Europe, remember?"

"Oh, yeah." She'd made that mistake when her mom first told her about going on this trip. She must be really, really, *really* TIRED to make that mistake again. Brooke looked around to see if anyone had heard her. If they did, they were too sleepy to laugh at her. "I remember now. Austria is next to Germany."

"And Italy." Mrs. Mason gently rubbed Brooke's back. "Instead of pictures of kangaroos, we'll get a picture of you in a castle."

"Oh, yeah. Castles! I remember now."

"Next," the man in the little booth said.

"That's us," Brooke's mom said.

Brooke tried to stop a monster yawn. She stood up and pulled her suitcase up to the booth. She handed her passport to the customs agent.

"How long will you be in Austria?" the man asked. He looked tired too. She wondered if it felt like 2:42 in the morning for him.

"Two weeks," Mrs. Mason said.

The man stamped their passports. Bam, bam. "And what will you be doing here?" he asked.

"I'm an art expert. I've been invited to help a man organize his large collection of American paintings," Mrs. Mason explained. Brooke was proud her mom was an authority on art. She was lucky enough to come with her mom. Her two brothers had to stay home, so Brooke felt doubly lucky.

"And will you be working too, Miss Mason?" the immigration agent asked.

"No, sir. I'm only nine-years old. I get to have fun."

The tired man in the booth laughed and stamped their passports again. Bam, bam. "Well, Miss Brooke Mason, I hope you do have fun. Welcome to Austria."

Austria. *Not* Australia. Brooke was going to

have to remember that! She followed closely behind her mom. She didn't want to get lost before they even started.

When they got outside of customs, Mrs. Mason stopped and looked around. Brooke plunked down on her suitcase again.

"*Herr* Mueller should be here soon," Mrs. Mason said. "Our flight was a few minutes early."

"Hair Mueller?" Brooke said. "What kind of a goofy name is Hair?"

Mrs. Mason laughed. "It sounds like 'hair,' but it's spelled H-E-R-R. It means mister in German."

"Oh, so we're looking for *Mr.* Mueller."

"Yes. But since we're in Austria, we'll call him Herr Mueller, won't we?" Mrs. Mason gave Brooke a no-nonsense look. She looked tired too.

"Why do they speak German here? Since we're in Austria, shouldn't we speak Austrian?"

Mrs. Mason thought for a minute. "Well, we're

Americans but we don't speak 'American.' We speak English because English speaking people colonized America. The people who settled Germany and Austria spoke a common language."

"That makes sense. So how do you say 'Mrs.' in German?"

"*Frau*. I'm Frau Mason."

"And me?"

"You, young lady, are a *Fräulein*. Fräulein Mason."

"I like that," she said and smiled.

Brooke scanned the room. She decided that Austrians looked a lot like people in Colorado. They came in all shapes and sizes. They were dressed like people would dress at the airport in Denver. She relaxed a little. Most people looked like they were waiting for someone.

One man, though, marched straight towards them. He had a long, thin face, a mouth bent into

a frown, and a bony body. A tangle of crazy grey
eyebrows shadowed his icy blue eyes and
mean mouth.

Brooke immediately decided she didn't like
him. She didn't even want to be in the same
room with this man. In fact, it
was more than that. Something
about his face and his stride
spooked her. Without
thinking, she reached up to
her mom's hand for a
little comfort. As soon
as he passed, she'd
be fine.

Only he
didn't pass. He
stopped right
in front of
Brooke and

her mom. "Frau Mason?" he asked. He held out his hand. "*Grüß Gott!* I'm Herr Mueller. Welcome to Austria."

Chapter Two

Schloss Mueller

At least Brooke didn't say, "Yikes!"

Well, at least she didn't say it out loud. She certainly said it inside her head. No way did she want to spend two weeks with this man.

Mrs. Mason smiled and said, "I'm pleased to meet you, Herr Mueller." She turned toward Brooke and squeezed her hand a little. That was Brooke's signal to say polite things and shake Herr Mueller's hand, which was the last—

the very last—thing she wanted to do. She did it anyway.

"How do you do, Herr Mueller?" Brooke's stomach turned upside down. She didn't lie, though, and say, "I'm pleased to meet you."

Herr Mueller smiled at Brooke. It didn't help. *"Guten Tag, Fräulein. Ich freue mich, Sie zu treffen."*

Brooke's mom leaned down and whispered in her ear. "He says he's pleased to meet you."

Brooke should have felt better, but she didn't.

"My car is parked close. Let me help you with your luggage." Without giving them a chance to respond, Herr Mueller took both her mom's suitcase handle and Brooke's and quickly wheeled the suitcases behind him. He looked a tiny bit less scary pulling Brooke's suitcase covered with galloping horses.

A tiny bit.

They were headed to Kitzbühel, Austria.

Schloss Mueller

Brooke knew that much. Her mom had shown her where the little town was on the map. Herr Mueller lived near Kitzbühel in a place called Schloss Mueller. Brooke's mom pronounced the word kind of like "shlose." She told her that *Schloss* was the German word for castle. Brooke couldn't wait to see it. She would be living in a castle for two whole weeks! Her friends would be so jealous.

She just wished scary Herr Mueller didn't have to stay in the castle too.

"Kitzbühel is just like one of our mountain ski towns," Mrs. Mason explained before they ever left Colorado.

That was mostly true. As they drove the winding roads, the wildly green hills reminded Brooke of Colorado mountains in the spring. In the distance, rugged peaks poked up in between the valleys. The towns looked different though.

The houses looked so much alike that the same person could have designed them all.

Brooke's mom must have noticed this too. "The houses all look similar."

Herr Mueller nodded. "It's the tradition in this region. The houses are white with red roofs. We have laws about the shape and slope of the roof and the house style in general. That's why the houses look so much the same. We like this look."

Brooke had to agree it was pretty. She tried to imagine what people in Colorado would say if everyone's house looked so much alike. As attractive as it was, though, she was pretty sure most Americans would still prefer a variety of house styles.

The drive to Kitzbühel zipped by fast. Or at least it seemed that way to Brooke since she slept most of the way. She woke up just as they pulled into Kitzbühel. The little village was postcard pretty. Cherry red flowers tumbled from window boxes on the houses. A great stone church towered above the town. Its bells sang the hour as they drove through the narrow cobblestone streets.

Just after the church, Herr Mueller turned and headed up the mountain on a twisting road. The town grew smaller below them. Even though Brooke was still a little nervous about Herr Mueller, she wasn't afraid of the drive. She'd been on lots of mountain roads in Colorado. She knew houses could shrink below them till they looked like toy houses.

Finally, they turned onto a wide paved lane. Perfectly cut hedges lined both sides. The hedges reached so high Brooke felt like they were in a cozy green tunnel. At the last curve, Herr Mueller's castle, or *Schloss,* appeared.

"Yikes!" Brooke said. This time she said it

out loud. She knew because both Herr Mueller and her mom turned around and looked at her. She couldn't help it though. Schloss Mueller—which looked more like a giant hotel—towered over them. The pale stone and long thin windows somehow matched Herr Mueller. "This is big enough for my whole soccer team and their families," Brooke said.

Herr Mueller had a sad smile. "Yes, *Fräulein*. Unfortunately, except for the housekeeper and the boy who takes care of the garden and horses, only my granddaughter and I live here now."

At that moment, the ancient front door creaked open. A thin, blond-haired girl in pink ballerina tights and slippers poked her head out. *"Grossvater!"*

"Eva!" Herr Mueller said. His face brightened into a real smile for the first time that day.

Schloss Mueller

Mrs. Mason and Brooke climbed out of the car.

"Frau Mason, *Fräulein*, this is my granddaughter, Eva. She's nine, just like you," Herr Mueller said.

"How do you do, Eva," Mrs. Mason said.

"Hi," Brooke said. "It's nice to meet you." Eva looked like the opposite of Brooke. Brooke had long straight black hair. Eva's was blond and curly. Brooke was short and, as her mother liked to say, solid. Eva was tall and thin in all the places a girl could be thin. Brooke had skin the color of a roasted peanut. Eva's skin was creamy white, like the inside of an apple.

But they did share one thing in common. They both had big, friendly smiles.

"Welcome to Schloss Mueller," Eva said in perfect English. "I'm so glad you're here." She did a small curtsey. Then she turned to her grandfather and, still in English, said, "Grandfather, while you were gone, the ballerina ghost returned!"

Chapter Three

Eva's Ballerina Room

"Ghost?" Brooke whispered to her mom. "Maybe there's a hotel in town."

Herr Mueller's smile turned back upside down. "Eva," he said softly. *"Bitte. Jetzt ist nicht die Zeit."*

Brooke was curious about what he must have said. Eva didn't look any happier than her grandfather.

Herr Mueller turned to Brooke's mom. "I must apologize. Eva has a vivid imagination."

Mrs. Mason looked a little nervous, but she smiled. "All little girls should have a good imagination, Herr Mueller." She squeezed Brooke's hand again.

The old man nodded and said, "Of course." But Brooke thought he looked a little sad. "Eva, don't you need to return to your ballet lesson? I'm sure Frau Thaler is waiting."

"Yes, Grandfather. But may I show Brooke her room first?"

Herr Mueller sighed. "Of course, *Liebling*. I know you won't be able to think about dancing until you do."

Eva's blue eyes sparkled. "Come with me! You get to sleep in my room." She took Brooke's hand and the girls ran up the broad stone steps and into Schloss Mueller.

"Wow!" Brooke said. "This is humongous!" She stopped and stared. The entry seemed as big as a house itself. The ceiling rose above them all the way to the roof. At the peak, a glittery chandelier hung down a full story. A stairway curved along the wall, rising up three full floors.

"Yes," Eva agreed. "It's too big if you ask me. I could hide from Grandfather forever if I wanted to." Brooke liked that idea. If she needed to, *she* could hide from the old man.

Eva tugged on Brooke's hand. "Let's go up to my room." The girls ran up the stairs to the first floor. Brooke stopped for another minute to look down over the rail. From up here she could see the floor. The wood had been laid out in a delicate design with angles and swirls.

"Can you see the ballerina?" Eva whispered.

Brooke jumped back. "The ghost?" she squeaked.

"Silly. Not the ballerina ghost," Eva said. "The ballerina in the floor design. See?" She drew an outline in the air over the floor.

"She's doing a pirouette."

"A pirouette? What's that?" Brooke asked.

"It's when a dancer spins on one leg."

Brooke tilted her head slightly. "I can see her!"

"My grandmother was a famous Austrian ballerina. After she married Grandfather, she quit dancing. He had the floor created for her. She always loved to dance. She was as graceful as a flying bird." Eva stepped back from the rail and twirled on her toes. She looked as light as a bird herself. "Someday, I'll be a famous ballerina too."

"Eva?" a woman called up from below. *Wo bist du?*

Eva sighed. *Eine Minute, Frau Thaler.* She turned to Brooke and whispered, "It's my ballet teacher. She's very impatient."

Of course she was. As far as Brooke was concerned, most adults were.

"Here it is," Eva said and pulled Brooke down

the hall and into a bedroom. "Do you like it?" She twirled again. "It's a ballerina's room."

Brooke never was and never would be a ballerina. She was more of a horse girl herself. But she loved the room anyway. Pink curtains framed the window. Fluffy lavender pillows covered the comfy bed and the rocking chair beside it. A shelf full of dolls in ballet costumes lined one wall. A couple of them looked as big as a real girl. The lower shelves held books and games. Best of all, a playhouse took up one whole corner of the room. It looked a little like Schloss Mueller, only happier somehow.

"It's a room for a princess!" Brooke said at last. She could hardly believe she would be living in this room for two whole weeks.

Eva laughed. "Not a princess you silly girl. A ballerina!" She danced out of the room and called back. "See you at dinner. I have to go back to my ballet lesson."

And then she was gone.

Brooke stood there a few minutes more. How lucky could a girl get? And then she remembered the ghost. The ballerina ghost. What better place for a ghost to hang out than in a ballerina room?

Yikes!

Brooke took one last look at the room and then raced back downstairs to find her mom.

Chapter Four

The Ghostly Visit

Dinner was something else.

The four of them—Herr Mueller, Eva, Mrs. Mason, and Brooke—sat at a table big enough for 16 people. They had that much food too, but they didn't eat it all.

Herr Mueller sat at one end and Brooke's mom at the other. Eva and Brooke sat in the middle facing each other. But with all the candles and the flowers and the glasses and the food, there didn't seem to be much room for conversation. It didn't feel at all like dinner with her family in Colorado.

In fact, for the first time, maybe ever (that's with a lower case *e*), Brooke missed her brothers. They always had a goofy story to tell about school or soccer. Her dad had an endless supply of funny jokes. Most of the time, she didn't laugh. She groaned.

Dinner at the Mason house was happy and noisy.

The only noise now was the silverware and glasses and Frau Eder, the cook, bringing in more food or taking dishes away. Mrs. Mason asked about the castle and Herr Mueller's art collection. Mostly it was boring adult talk.

Mrs. Mason also asked about Eva's English. "Eva, where did you learn to speak such good English?"

Brooke nodded. "You speak better than most of the kids I go to school with."

They all laughed, but it was true.

"It's not so good, really," Eva said even though it was very good. She blushed. "Before I started first grade, I lived in California for a year. My dad worked there. Now my parents travel all the time for business."

"Well, not all the time, *Liebling.*" Herr Mueller waved his fork at her.

"Anyway, we all live with Grandfather." She looked tiny at the long table that stretched on both sides of her. "I keep working on my English though. I have a tutor who comes twice a week."

"You're a lucky girl to be able to speak two languages so well!" Mrs. Mason said. Herr Mueller smiled at his granddaughter. "She's a lucky girl in many ways."

Eva smiled. But she didn't look happy.

Frau Eder had prepared carrot soup and beet salad. Next came *Spätzle*, which was like fat noodles, and *Wiener Schnitzel* with lemon wedges and cranberry sauce. It was not just yummy. It was Yummy! Brooke caught the sweet, buttery scent of dessert before she saw it. The skillet-sized pancake with apples, nuts, and raisins was Double Yummy!

"What's this called?" Brooke asked.

"*Kaiserschmarrn*," Eva said. "It's the special dessert of Austria."

"Kizer shmarn?" Brooke said. She tried to copy how it sounded.

"Close enough," Herr Mueller said.

Brooke loved the *Kaiserschmarrn*. She asked for seconds and thirds, but then she saw the look on her mom's face. She didn't ask for fourths. She would have if she could have, though.

But she did ask if her mom could have the recipe.

After dinner, Herr Mueller and Brooke's mom had coffee in a small room with lots of books.

They talked about Herr Mueller's paintings. Herr Mueller gave Eva and Brooke permission to leave.

"Is it always that quiet at dinner?" Brooke asked as they climbed the stairs. She thought maybe she and her mom should have talked more.

"That quiet?" Eva said. "Usually, it's even worse. Tonight was fun."

The girls went up to Eva's room. Eva showed Brooke her favorite dolls. Then they organized the playhouse and pretended to be two princesses. Eva, of course, pretended to be a ballerina princess. Brooke didn't want to be an ordinary princess, so she was a famous horse-riding princess.

And that's how Mrs. Mason would have found them. Except the famous horse-riding princess had traveled a long way that day. She was already sound asleep on the ballerina princess' floor.

Mrs. Mason helped Brooke slip into her

pajamas and climb into bed. She kissed her good night. Brooke was so sleepy she hardly remembered any of it.

What she did remember was waking up to Eva shaking her violently.

"I saw her! I saw the ballerina ghost again!" she whispered urgently.

Eva flipped on the light switch.

Brooke didn't see anything except the rocking chair next to the bed.

It was moving back and forth like someone was rocking it. Only no one sat in the chair.

Instead, there was a pink ballet slipper on the seat.

Chapter Five

The Face in the Window

"Who is the ballerina ghost? And why is she haunting Schloss Mueller?" Brooke finally asked Eva.

The two girls had packed a small picnic lunch and were out riding through emerald green pastures. Black and white cows grazed everywhere. Cowbells clanged and clinked. Brooke liked the sound. It was a crisp June morning. The sweet scent of grass and pine trees reminded Brooke of summer in

Colorado. Out in all this sunshine and away from Schloss Mueller, Brooke finally had the nerve to ask Eva about the ghost.

The night before, when the ballerina ghost rocked the chair, Brooke could only hide under her covers. She thought she'd never sleep again. But it

seemed like minutes later and the sun was up.

Eva sighed. "I think the ghost is Rose. She was the little sister of my great-grandfather. They say she died of influenza way back in 1917." Eva glanced around as though she thought someone might be listening. Then she whispered, "I don't think she really died of influenza. I think she died of loneliness." She nodded in a self-assured way. "And now she's looking for a little girl to play with."

"Loneliness?" Brooke asked. She didn't believe it. "How could she be lonely here? There must have been cooks and maids and gardeners then. And stable boys." Brooke thought of the cute boy who had helped them saddle their horses. She wished she had a stable boy at home. But nope. She only had brothers.

Eva tilted her head and squinted an eye at Brooke. "You think you can't be lonely if people are around you?" She shook her head. "You can be surrounded by cooks and dance teachers and stable boys. And you can still be very, very lonely."

She muttered something else. To Brooke it sounded like, "Just look at me." But she wasn't sure.

"Aren't you afraid of her?" Brooke asked.

"Afraid?" Eva said thoughtfully. "No. Not really. Startled maybe, but not truly scared."

Brooke's heart had pounded the night before. Even if she believed Eva wasn't afraid—and she didn't—Brooke had been scared stiff.

"Why not?" she asked Eva. "A ghost is a ghost."

"Because a lonely girl would never hurt someone she wants to be friends with."

"Maybe not on purpose, but I came pretty close to being scared to death last night!"

"You get used to her. She's friendly," Eva

insisted. She saw the look on Brooke's face. "Really. It's true."

Brooke thought her new friend was a good storyteller.

Eva rode a rust-colored horse and Brooke a black one. It reminded Brooke of her own horse, Snowflake, back in Colorado. She had just enough spirit to be fun, but not so much that Brooke had to pay a lot of attention. She was secretly happy to see that she was better with horses than Eva. Much better.

The two girls rode in silence for a while. They trotted along a crystal stream as it splashed through a narrow valley. Bouquets of tiny white flowers grew like cloud puffs along the banks.

Late morning, the girls stopped for lunch. Eva unpacked a lip-smacking picnic that Frau Eder had made for them. They had salami on hard rolls, pickles, and potato salad (but not like the potato salad

Brooke knew since this was *just* potatoes and a clear dressing). For dessert they had chocolates. They weren't as sweet as the chocolates in Colorado. But Brooke could have eaten all of them herself anyway.

"This is super duper yummy," Brooke said between bites. "You're very lucky. You have someone to cook and clean and help you with the horses."

Eva picked a few pink flowers by her feet. "I don't think I'm so lucky," she said.

Brooke laughed. "Are you kidding? I'd give anything to live in a house like yours. It's so beautiful." She smiled at her new friend.

Eva didn't smile back. "Oh yes. It's great for a little while, maybe even a few weeks. But not for all the time."

"Why?"

"Because it's lonely, can't you see? Grandfather says he wants me to have the very best education.

So he hires a private teacher for me for school. And in the summer, he keeps me busy with lessons. Ballet on Monday and Friday. Horseback riding on Wednesday. English on Tuesday and Saturday."

"But it sounds like you spend lots of time

with people."

Eva paused a moment. Then she said, "People, yes. But no one is my age." Now Eva smiled. Her blue eyes grew bright and happy. "That's why I'm so glad you're here!"

It made Brooke feel warm inside. She liked Eva.

They cleaned up their lunch and got back on their horses. Then they headed back toward Schloss Mueller.

When they crossed a walking path, a family of hikers waved to them. They didn't look like hikers in Colorado. They looked more like they were going to a costume party. The father and son were dressed in leather shorts and suspenders. They both had red kerchiefs around their necks. The mother and daughter both wore dresses with aprons.

"Why are they dressed like that?" Brooke asked when she didn't think the family could hear.

"Like what?" Eva asked.

"In those shorts and suspenders. And the dresses and aprons. At home, people never dress like that when they go out walking."

"Oh, you mean the *Lederhosen*. It means leather trousers. The girls are wearing a *Dirndl* and an apron. That's the traditional dress for this part of Austria. We're very proud of our past. So that's one way we keep it alive. Most of the time we do not dress up for a hike. The family must be having a special day. How do you dress for hiking in Colorado?"

Brooke thought for a moment. "Shorts and t-shirts if it's summer. We dress in a more casual way."

Eva laughed. "We dress like that too. But it's nice to have a tradition, don't you think?"

Brooke didn't say anything. She had a hard time thinking of any Colorado traditions.

"Austria has lots of traditions. We've been

making them for hundreds and hundreds of years. Some of the traditions go back to when the Romans and Celts were here. That was nearly 2000 years ago. How old is Colorado?" Eva asked.

Brooke knew the answer to that. She had studied Colorado history in school. "The Utes and Cheyenne Indians lived there a long time before it was settled. But as a state, we're only about 150 years old."

Eva laughed. "My *house* is over 400 years old. One hundred fifty years? That's nothing. It takes a long time to make a tradition."

Brooke thought about that. She was sure Colorado had traditions. The Broncos were a tradition. But a football team didn't seem to count, especially if she thought about what would last hundreds of years. Thanksgiving was a tradition. And watching fireworks on 4th of July. But those were things everyone in America celebrated.

"Well, we wear cowboy hats and boots when we ride horses," Brooke said. "That's a Colorado tradition like your *Lederhosen* and *Dirndl.*" She was happy she'd thought of something that made Colorado special like Austria.

A few clouds drifted lazily above. All around them the day burst with color. The path turned and Schloss Mueller came into view. Even it was colorful. In each window, bright pink, white, and yellow flowers overflowed from flower boxes. The pale stone sparkled in the afternoon sun. Brooke decided it couldn't be a more perfect day.

That thought lasted 30 seconds.

"Oh no!" Eva whispered. "Look!" She pointed at the castle.

Brooke's stomach turned upside down. She had goose bumps. Only it wasn't cold.

"Wh-where?" she stuttered. She didn't want to see whatever it was.

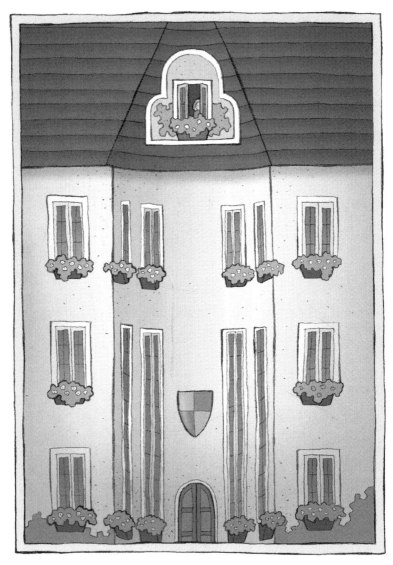

"There! Look at the attic window,"
Eva insisted.

Brooke looked where Eva pointed. A blond-
haired little girl stared out at the mountains.

"It's the ballerina ghost!"

Chapter Six

The Note

Eva spurred her horse. She flew toward Schloss Mueller. "Come on! We've got to catch her!"

Brooke coaxed her horse to follow even though she certainly didn't want to catch any ghost. By the time she reached the castle, Eva had already jumped off her horse and raced inside.

Brooke was torn. Ghost or no ghost, she wanted to follow her friend. But at home, she would never just jump off her horse and leave it—

unless she wanted to get grounded. At that moment, Kurt, the stable boy appeared.

"Is okay. I take care of horse," he said.

"Really?" Brooke loved this stable boy more than ever.

"*Ja, ja.* Is okay. Go *mit* Eva." He smiled, but he sighed, too.

"Thanks! I owe you a big one," Brooke yelled over her shoulder.

She took three steps at a time. First floor. Second floor. Third floor. Her side ached, but she couldn't stop.

Above her, she could hear Eva calling. "Brooke! Brooke! Hurry up!"

Brooke looked all around her. She knew there was one more story to go. But she couldn't see more steps.

To her left, she heard a clatter. Brooke froze. She didn't want to meet the ballerina ghost! But it was Eva who poked her head out into the wide hall. She waved Brooke over. "Come on!"

Brooke scooted after her and up the last flight of steps.

"Is she . . . is the ghost up here?" she asked. She wasn't sure she wanted to know the answer.

"No," Eva said. She sounded disappointed. "But look at what I found." She held up a pink ribbon. "It's the kind of ribbon I tie my ballet slipper with."

"Yikes!" Brooke said. She wanted to say a few other words. But if her mom ever found out, she'd spend the next two weeks sitting right next to her mom and a pile of paintings.

Eva headed over to the window where the blond ghost had been. A rocking chair and a small table sat next to the window. "And look over here," she said. "There's a note." She pointed to a piece of paper. "Look what it says."

The Note

Please be my Frend,
Rose

"See?" Eva said. "I told you it's Rose. The ghost *is* my great-grandfather's sister. And see? She just wants a friend."

Brooke took a deep breath. She was shaking, partly from the climb, but mostly because of what she was thinking.

"Eva. For us to be the friend of a ghost, wouldn't we have to be . . ." she paused. She couldn't quite bring herself to say the words. "Wouldn't we have to be dead?"

Chapter Seven

The Note Disappears

At the foot of the attic stairs, the door slammed.

Both girls screamed and jumped. Brooke was running before she landed.

"Yikes! I'm outta' here!" she yelled as she ran.

Eva was two steps behind her. They clattered down flight after flight of stairs and straight to the library where Mrs. Mason was working.

The girls' words tumbled out and over each other as they tried to explain what had just happened.

The Note Disappears

"We saw the ghost!"

"In the window in the attic —"

"She left a pink ballerina ribbon—"

"And a note—"

"She wants to be our friend—"

"That's what the note said—"

"But wouldn't we have to be dead to be her friend?"

"And then the door slammed!"

"Hold on, hold on," Mrs. Mason said. "What are you girls trying to tell me? You saw the ghost?" She put down the painting she was working with.

"The ballerina ghost!" Eva said.

Mrs. Mason took the girls' hands and led them to a soft leather couch. "Now just sit down and tell me what happened."

They started telling the story again in their crazy way.

Mrs. Mason held up her hand. "One at a time.

Please." She looked at Brooke. "Take a deep breath. Now what happened?"

Once more, Brooke began. Eva interrupted to add details. But she only did it two times, so Mrs. Mason let her.

When Brooke finished, Mrs. Mason shook her head. "That sounds like a wild story. Let's go up to the attic and take a look."

Brooke was horrified. "NO WAY! There's a ghost up there!"

Mrs. Mason said, "Well, there are three of us. And there's only one ghost. Let's see what we can find out."

The girls looked at each other. That was the *last* thing they wanted to do. But Mrs. Mason took their hands and marched up, up, up until they reached the attic.

The pink ribbon still lay on the floor where Eva had dropped it when the door slammed.

But the note was gone.

"Really, Mom," Brooke said. "There was a note from the ghost."

"Well, maybe it blew out the window." Mrs. Mason walked over and shut the window by the rocking chair. "That's probably what made the attic door slam too. This was open so there was a draft."

"That might explain why the door slammed and why there's no note. But it doesn't explain why there was a note in the first place," Brooke said.

Mrs. Mason had a look on her face that

Brooke couldn't quite figure out.

"It's the truth, Mrs. Mason," Eva said. "We both saw the note."

Mrs. Mason chewed on her lip. "I don't know what's going on. When Herr Mueller gets back, we'll ask him what he thinks."

Eva sighed and muttered, "Now I'll be in *real* trouble."

Chapter Eight

The Scent of Roses

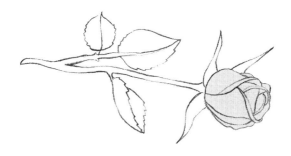

When Herr Mueller returned home, he was in a good mood. Once he heard the story, though, he was in a bad mood.

He and Eva talked softly in German. They could have talked loudly for all the German Brooke and her mom knew. It looked like a serious, unhappy talk.

When the girls were alone again, Eva said, "He doesn't believe me. He says I'm making everything up." She wiped away a tear.

"But we saw her in the window!" Brooke said. "And we saw the note!" She decided her first impression of Herr Mueller was the right one. He was a mean old man.

"I know. But he still doesn't believe me."

"But how can you prove a ghost to your grandfather?" Brooke asked.

"Maybe we can find more clues in the attic," Eva said.

"You're crazy! You think I'm willing to go back up there?" Brooke said. "Not a chance."

The girls drifted out to the garden behind the house. Eva wanted to pretend they were famous ballerinas. The garden flowers were really people in the audience. A bad witch had turned them into roses and lilies.

"If I dance," Eva said, "I'll forget I'm mad at Grandfather."

The Scent of Roses

Brooke didn't feel like dancing. Her stomach felt all twisted up. She had this funny feeling the ghost was looking at her. But every time she looked up at the attic window, it was empty. So while Eva twirled and leaped, Brooke wandered through the flowers.

"That's good, Brooke," Eva said between twirls. "If you smell the right one, you'll break the wicked spell. You'll turn them all back into people."

Brooke was perfectly happy sniffing instead of dancing. She liked the roses best. They grew in orderly clumps of pink, yellow, or red. Brooke bent over to smell a pink one with a big white petal.

Only the white wasn't part of the flower after all. It was a piece of paper. Brooke picked it out of the flower just as Herr Mueller called to the girls.

"Would you girls like to go for ice cream?"

"Of course!" Eva called back. She turned to Brooke and whispered so her grandfather wouldn't hear. "Ice cream will make all of us feel better." Then she twirled off toward the house.

Brooke put the paper into her pocket and dashed after her friend. She was never one to turn down ice cream.

The girls ran upstairs to clean up. When Brooke came out of the bathroom, Eva had a funny look on her face.

"What's wrong?" Brooke asked.

"Wrong?" Eva said. "Nothing." But the funny look stayed on her face.

"Did you see the ballerina ghost again?" Brooke asked. Her stomach flopped upside down.

"No. I was just—"

"Girls," Herr Mueller called up the stairs. "Are you ready yet?"

"Coming, Grandfather," Eva called back. She flew out of the room before Brooke could say another word.

Something didn't seem quite right to Brooke, but she couldn't put her finger on what it was.

Brooke's mom decided she'd take a break too. She joined them in the car for the ride down the mountain. No one said a word about the ghost. But Brooke couldn't stop thinking about the face in the window. She wondered, too, what was up with Eva. She would have to remember to ask her later.

Herr Mueller parked the car on a cobblestone street crowded with cars and people. The four of them walked through a giant stone arch where only people could go. Cafés with tables outside lined the street. At the end of the street, an old stone church seemed to float above the village. Its bell tower touched the sky.

"This is the original village," Herr Mueller said. "Now it's a place to shop and eat. A long time ago, though, this is where everyone worked and lived."

"It's so quaint," Mrs. Mason said. "I love all the flowers in the window boxes."

Brooke liked the street too. It didn't look anything like the wide streets of her small Colorado town. There the buildings were only one or two stories. And they all looked different. Here the structures looked like they had been planned by the same person. A horse-drawn carriage passed by them.

"Is this how people still travel in Austria?" Brooke asked. As soon as she said it, she felt silly. She knew people used cars there just like at home.

Herr Mueller chuckled. "No. But we know the tourists who come like such things." He smiled at her and didn't seem quite so mean. He led them to a café where the tables had cheerful red and white striped umbrellas.

Herr Mueller ordered scoops of ice cream for everyone. Brooke thought it tasted like ice cream at home, only better. Above them, the church bells sang. Brooke counted four gongs at the end.

She tried to take a picture in her mind of the moment. But she wanted to remember more than what she saw. She wanted to remember the church

bells clanging and the horse's hooves clopping on the street. She wanted to remember the fruity taste of the ice cream and the earthy smell of the geraniums in the window boxes. She wanted to remember the warm sunny day and the fun she was having with her new friend.

After they finished the ice cream, the girls passed a little shop with a window display of friendship bracelets. Eva tugged Brooke inside. Each of them picked out a bracelet for the other one. Eva found a lavender one with ballerina slippers to give to Brooke. Brooke chose a pink one with silver hearts for Eva.

"We're friends forever," Eva said.

Next door was a tiny toy store tucked away under a stone stairway. Dolls of every kind shared the shelves with blue and yellow wooden trains and trucks. Mrs. Mason picked a doll out for Brooke that had a costume like the girl they saw hiking with her family. The doll had blue eyes, blond hair, and rosy cheeks.

"I'm going to name her Eva," Brooke said. "It's the perfect name for a perfect doll."

The girls took turns holding Eva as they walked back to the car. The day had turned out to be a happy one. Brooke decided nothing could change that.

Herr Mueller unlocked the car. The girls climbed in the back seat where the sun had made the air warm. "Do you smell something?" Eva asked.

Brooke sniffed. "I do. What's that smell?"

Mrs. Mason sniffed the air too. "It's roses, isn't it?"

"Roses?" Eva stiffened. "Rose! That's the name of the ballerina ghost!"

Brooke shuddered. Her skin tingled with goose bumps. The ghost knew they'd left the castle and had followed them!

Chapter Nine

No More Chances!

"Eva," Herr Mueller said. It sounded a lot like a sigh.

Mrs. Mason looked nervous.

Brooke *felt* nervous.

Only Eva had a small smile on her face.

No one talked during the ride back up the twisting mountain road. When they reached Schloss Mueller, though, Mrs. Mason had an announcement.

"Herr Mueller, this has been a wonderful trip. However, I have to admit I'm frightened by this ghost." She looked at Brooke. "I think it's time we leave."

"No!" Eva said. "The ghost is friendly. She only wants to play with us. She won't hurt anyone, I promise."

"I'm sorry, Eva," Mrs. Mason said. "I think this is best."

Eva burst into tears. She ran inside and up to her room.

"I'm very sorry, Herr Mueller," Mrs. Mason said. "I'll give you a report of the work I've done so far." She turned to Brooke. "Honey, go pack your bags. I'll call to change our flight."

Brooke felt sad to leave Eva. But she was also relieved not to stay anymore in a castle with a ghost. She headed up the stairs.

When she got to Eva's room, her friend was

sitting on the bed and crying. "I don't want you to go."

"I don't want to leave you, Eva," Brooke said. "But I'm scared of the ghost too." She felt sad inside. Then she got a great idea. "Maybe you could come visit me in Colorado."

"That would be fun," Eva said. She smiled a little even though the tears kept running down her cheeks.

Brooke put her things in her suitcase and carried her new doll and the suitcase downstairs. Mrs. Mason stood at the bottom of the stairs. She and Herr Mueller talked quietly with each other. When they saw Brooke, they stopped talking.

"Eva," Herr Mueller called up the stairs. "It's time for Brooke and Frau Mason to leave. Do you want to ride with us?"

"Yes, Grandfather," Eva called down. "I'm coming."

No More Chances

A minute later she came running down the stairs. In her hand she had a doll. It had blue eyes and blond hair and wore a pink ballerina skirt. It was almost as big as Brooke. "Here. I want you to have my ballerina doll. I want you to always remember Austria." She looked like she was going to cry again. "And me."

"Eva," Mrs. Mason said. "That's very kind of you."

"I wrote you a goodbye letter too," Eva said. She handed it to Brooke.

Brooke read it out loud:

Dear Brooke,

Thank you for being my frend. I hope we get to see each other again.

your Frend
Eva

She looked at the letter from Eva. There was something about it that didn't seem quite right. She looked at the writing and the spelling. And then she remembered something.

Brooke took the piece of paper out of her

pocket that she had found in the garden that afternoon. It was the note from the ballerina ghost. She looked at the two pieces of paper. Each one had the same misspelled word. Each one had the same writing. Suddenly Brooke knew who the ballerina ghost was.

"Eva! It's you."

"What do you mean?"

"You're the ballerina ghost."

"What?" Eva said. "No!"

"You wrote both of these notes." Brooke held up the doll Eva had just given her. "And this doll looks just like the ghost in the attic window."

"No! I just—"

"Eva," Herr Mueller said. "Is this true?"

Eva burst into tears.

Brooke wanted to cry too. "I'm sorry, Eva. It's just that the notes look like the same person wrote them both." She hated to see her friend cry.

If she could only find another way to explain it.

"Eva?" Herr Mueller said. He sounded sad too. "Did you write both notes?"

The little girl nodded slowly.

"Why did you do this?" Herr Mueller asked.

Eva couldn't talk, though, because she was sobbing loudly.

Mrs. Mason leaned down and hugged Eva.

Brooke took a deep breath. She said, "I think I know why she pretended there was a ghost."

"You do?" Herr Mueller asked.

Brooke nodded. "I think Eva is the one who wants a friend." She smiled at Eva.

Eva wiped her cheeks. She nodded slightly.

"But she has many friends," Herr Mueller said.

Brooke took a deep breath. Herr Mueller still scared her but not as much. "She has friends, Herr Mueller. But she doesn't have any time to play with them."

"Brooke, that makes a lot of sense. This is a big house to live in," Mrs. Mason said. "And you're so busy with all your lessons, Eva."

"But it's important she does her lessons," Herr Mueller said. "She needs to study ballet. She must keep up her English! And her horse riding lessons are important. She needs these things to grow up to be a successful young lady."

"I think she needs to have some fun too," Brooke said. "Tell us, Eva. Why did you make up the ghost story?"

Eva stopped sniffling. "It's true. I thought if Grandfather believed me, he would let me play with other children more. And maybe I wouldn't have to take so many lessons in the summer. I didn't mean to scare anyone away. I told Grandfather about a ghost before you ever came. I told him I thought it was Rose and she died of loneliness."

"But why did you keep up the ghost story when

I came?" Brooke asked.

Eva looked down at the floor. "I thought if you thought there was a ghost, then Grandfather would believe me." She looked at Brooke. "I never, ever wanted to scare you away."

"So there's no ghost at all?" Brooke asked.

Eva shook her head.

"What about when the rocking chair moved in the middle of the night?"

"I shook you to wake you up. Then I threw the shoe at the rocking chair and turned on the light. Because I said it was the ghost, you had a ghost on your mind."

"And how did you get the doll into the attic and write the note? We were out riding horseback together all morning."

"I did all that before you woke up. And then I ran fast up the stairs and hid the doll behind some boxes."

"And the smell of roses in the car?"

Eva pulled a small sachet out of her pocket. "I put it in my pocket when we went to clean up. That's why I had that funny look on my face when you came out of the bathroom. I thought you saw me. Then I left the sachet in the car. I knew it would make the car smell like roses." She looked sheepish.

Brooke laughed. "You might be a lonely girl, but I think you're also a smart girl."

Herr Mueller was the one to look sheepish now. "Eva, I'm so sorry. I thought giving you private lessons was doing the best thing for you. I never wanted you to be lonely."

He kneeled down beside his granddaughter and put his arms around her. He didn't look so scary anymore. "What can I do to make it up to you?"

"I want to go to school with the other children in town," she said.

Herr Mueller sighed. "Perhaps that would be best."

"And I don't want to take so many lessons in the summer."

"But what about ballet lessons?"

"Well, I'll always want to take ballet lessons,"

she said and huffed a little. "How else will I become a famous Austrian ballerina?"

"Just like your grandmother," Herr Mueller said and smiled. He kissed Eva's forehead.

"Just like my grandmother!" Eva hugged her grandfather.

Brooke tugged on her mom's arm. "Can't we stay like we'd first planned?"

Mrs. Mason winked at Herr Mueller. "I think we can stay a little longer—as long as Eva promises we won't have any more visits from ghosts!"

"I promise!" Eva said. She and Brooke laughed and ran back upstairs to unpack Brooke's bag.

Sneak Peek of Another Adventure
Mystery of the Secret Room

Chapter One

". . . acht, neun, zehn . . . Ich komme!"

Here I come.

Brooke could barely hear Eva's voice as it drifted up the stairs into the attic. She should be tucked away in a hiding place by now. But she was still frantically looking for a good spot. She carefully moved some boxes to crouch behind. A spider darted across the new empty space. She jumped back and whispered, "Yikes!"

Her heart pounded. Thump, thump, thump.

Did Eva hear her jump?

She held her breath and listened for her friend's footsteps on the stairs.

The only sound was the rain tap, tap, tapping

on the window. A door screeched opened on the floor below and Eva called in a singsongy voice. *"Wo bist du?"* Where are you? Brooke was happy her German was getting better. Eva had been teaching her phrases, which was a good thing. If she was going to spend time with her Austrian friend, she should be able to speak a little German.

It sounded like Eva had moved away from the attic door. That gave her a few more minutes to hide. But where?

The cluttered room had a gazillion dark corners and even more shadows. White sheets covered furniture shapes. They seemed to glow in the grey afternoon light. If Brooke were cross-my-heart-hope-to-die honest, it was a little too spooky. Even though Eva's ballerina ghost had turned out to be a trick Eva played, Brooke still remembered how scary it was to see the "ghost" in the attic window. After all, if a ghost did live in Schloss Mueller, this dusty old space would be the perfect place for it to hang out.

Maybe she shouldn't have come up here to hide.

Too late now. She should have thought about this earlier. But she and Eva had hidden in all the good places already. The attic seemed like such a good idea when Brooke was on the floor below.

Where the windows were big.

And the noises were friendly.

And there weren't so many creepy, eepy shadows . . .

Find out what happens to Brooke and Eva in the Pack-n-Go Girls book, Mystery of the Secret Room.

Meet More Pack-n-Go Girls!

Discover Australia with Wendy and Chloe!

Mystery of the Min Min Lights
It's hot. It's windy. It's dusty. It's the
Australian outback. Wendy Lee arrives
from California. She's lucky to meet
Chloe Taylor, who invites Wendy to their
sheep station. It sounds like fun except
that someone is stealing the sheep. And
the thief just might be something as
crazy as a UFO.

Discover Brazil with Sofia and Júlia!

Mystery of the Troubled Toucan
Nine-year-old Sofia Diaz's world is coming
apart. So is the rickety old boat that carries
her far up the Rio Negro river in Brazil.
Crocodiles swim in the dark waters. Spiders
scurry up the twisted tree trunks. And a
crazy toucan screeches a warning. It chases Sofia and Júlia, her
new friend, deep into the steamy rainforest. There they stumble
upon a shocking discovery. Don't miss the second Brazil book,
Mystery of the Lazy Loggerhead.

Meet More Pack-n-Go Girls!

Discover Mexico with Izzy and Patti!

Mystery of the Thief in the Night

Izzy's family sails into a quiet lagoon in Mexico and drops their anchor. Izzy can't wait to explore the pretty little village, eat yummy tacos, and practice her Spanish. When she meets nine-year-old Patti, Izzy's thrilled. Now she can do all that and have a new friend to play with too. Life is perfect. At least it's perfect until they realize there's a midnight thief on the loose! Don't miss the second Mexico book, *Mystery of the Disappearing Dolphin*.

Discover Thailand with Jess and Nong May!

Mystery of the Golden Temple

Nong May and her family have had a lot of bad luck lately. When nine-year-old Jess arrives in Thailand and accidentally breaks a special family treasure, it seems to only get worse. It turns out the treasure holds a secret that could change things forever!

What to Know Before You Go!

Where is Austria?

Schoolchildren in Austria learn their country is shaped like a shoe. Can you see why they think that? Austria is in the southeastern area of Europe. It is completely surrounded by land. Austria has eight other countries as neighbors: Czech Republic, Germany, Hungary, Italy, Liechtenstein, Slovakia, Slovenia, and Switzerland. It's not a very big country. It's about the size of Maine. But it's a beautiful country full of forests and mountains. Because it has so many mountains, it's well known for its great skiing.

Facts about Austria

Official Name: Republic of Austria, which means "Eastern Empire" (the German name is Österreich)

Capital: Vienna (the German name is Wien)

Currency: Euro

Government: Parliamentary representative democracy

Language: Austrian German; this is very similar to German spoken in Germany

Population: 8,384,745 (2010)

Major Cities:
- Vienna: 1,523,000
- Graz: 219,000
- Linz: 185,000
- Salzburg: 145,000

Traveling in Austria

It's easy to travel in Austria. The roads and public transportation system are excellent. Many people speak English, so you can still go even if you don't speak German. If you go to Austria in the summer, take your walking shoes or plan to rent a bike. Austrians love to go hiking. If you go in the winter, don't forget your skis or snowboard. The Austrian mountains have some of the best skiing in the world. In fact, many Olympic skiers are from Austria.

What to Expect for Weather

Austria has three regions with three different climates. The eastern part of Austria is not mountainous. Temperatures range from an average high of 77° in July to an average low near 27° in January. Annual rainfall in this area is often less than 31 inches. The central region is where the mountains are. So the winters are long and wet. The mountains get lots of snow. The lower altitudes get rain. The temperature in the western part is cooler and wetter than in the east. It can get more than twice as much rain, but the July average high is only 79°. In January, the lows average near 20°.

What Austrians Eat

You won't have trouble finding familiar foods in Austria. Traditionally, though, Austrians eat meat and vegetables that are fried in a pan. A favorite dish is *Wiener Schnitzel*, which is a thin slice of veal coated in breadcrumbs and fried. Big dumplings are also common. Austria is also famous for *Kaiserschmarrn*. No doubt it got its name because the Austrian Emperor Franz Joseph loved it. The word "Kaiser" means king or emperor.

Recipe for Kaiserschmarrn

Ingredients *(If you make this recipe, be sure to get an adult to help you.):*

3 eggs	½ teaspoon vanilla	½ cup milk
½ cup flour	extract	½ cup butter
1 teaspoon sugar	½ teaspoon salt	raisins

1. Separate the egg yolks from the egg whites.

2. Mix the yolks, flour, sugar, vanilla extract, salt and milk into a batter.

3. Beat the egg whites until they are stiff. Mix it carefully with the batter.

4. Melt the butter in a pan and add the batter. Sprinkle some raisins over it and fry it on low heat. Turn the pancake over. Tear it in little pieces and fry through. Serve with powdered sugar and applesauce.

Say It in German!

English	German	German Pronunciation
Hello	Hallo	Hahl-lō
Hello (Good day)	Grüß Gott	Grōss gŏt
Good day	Guten Tag	Gū-těn tahg
Good morning	Guten Morgen	Gū-těn morgen
Good night	Guten Abend	Gū-těn ah-bend
Hi	Hi/Tag	Tahg
Goodbye	Auf Wiedersehen	Auf vē-der-zāhn
Bye	Tschuess	Tchoos
Please	Bitte	Bĭ-tah
Thank you (very much)	Danke (schön)/ (Vielen Dank)	Dahn-kah (feel-en dahnk)
Excuse me	Entschuldigen Sie mich	Ěnt-shū-lĭ-gěn zee mĭck
Yes/No	Ja/Nein	Yah/Nine
Enjoy the meal	Guten Appetit	Gū-těn a-pě-teet
Grandfather	Grossvater	Grōss vahter
Mrs./Miss	Frau/Fräulein	Frow/Frow-line
Mr.	Herr	Hair
Castle	Schloss	Shlōss
Sweetheart	Liebling	Leeb-Lĭng

84

English	German	German Pronunciation
When?	Wann?	Vahn
Why?	Warum?	Var-ūm
What?	Was?	Vahs
Who?	Wer?	Vair
Where?	Wo?	Vo
How?	Wie?	Vee
How much/many?	Wieviel/Wie viele?	Vee-fel/vee fēlah
Is/are there?	Gibt es?	Gĭbt ĕs
What is it?	Was ist das?	Vahs ist dahs
0	Null	Null
1	Eins	Īnz
2	Zwei	Zvī
3	Drei	Drī
4	Vier	Fear
5	Fünf	Funf
6	Sechs	Zĕchs
7	Sieben	Zēbĕn
8	Acht	Ahcht
9	Neun	Noin
10	Zehn	Zāne

Do you speak German? If so, you might notice *Herr* Mueller is used in some places where the correct German form is *Herrn* Mueller. So English readers aren't confused, Herr Mueller is used throughout as the character's name.

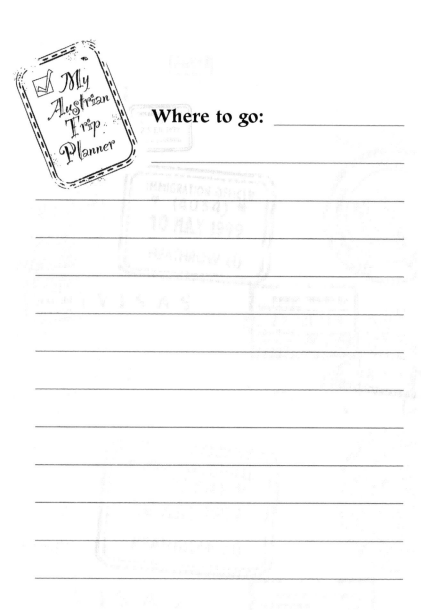

Where to go: _____

86

What to do:

My Austrian Trip Planner

My Austrian Trip Planner

Things I want to pack:

Friends to send postcards to:

My
Austrian
Trip
Planner

Thank you to the original Pack-n-Go Girls:

Emma Calarco

Alexis Carlson

Emily Chaston

Kaci Ferris

Anna James

Miranda Jenkins

Noel Martinez

Summer Mayes

Taylor O'Hare Heinicke

Hannah Lanakila Lewis

Erin Murphy

Olivia Sieders

Jane Sparks

Abigail Steffey

Anna Grace Warmack

Jasmine Wilkerson

Thank you also to:

Susan Bartel

Kate Bridgman

Caren Camhi

Olgy Gary

Althea Harvey

Karen Meenan

Stefan Pühringer

Andrea Rieger

Jeannie Sheeks

Missy Sieders

Elizabeth Stedem

Will Travis

Helene Wetzel

And a special thanks to my Pack-n-Go Girls co-founder, Lisa Travis, and our husbands, Steve Diller and Rich Travis, who have been along with us on this adventure.

Janelle Diller has always had a passion for writing. As a young child, she wouldn't leave home without a pad and pencil just in case her novel hit her and she had to scribble it down quickly. She eventually learned good writing takes a lot more time and effort than this. Fortunately, she still loves to write. She's especially lucky because she also loves to travel. She's explored over 45 countries for work and play and can't wait to land in the next new country. It doesn't get any better than writing stories about traveling. Janelle and her husband split their time between a sailboat in Mexico and a house in Colorado.

Adam Turner has been working as a freelance illustrator since 1987. He has illustrated coloring books, puzzle books, magazine articles, game packaging, and children's books. He's loved to draw ever since he picked up his first pencil as a toddler. Instead of doing the usual two-year-old thing of chewing on it or poking his eye out  with it, he actually put it on paper and thus began the journey. Adam also loves to travel and has had some crazy adventures. He's swum with crocodiles in the Zambezi, jumped out of a perfectly good airplane, and even fished for piranha in the Amazon. It's a good thing drawing relaxes his nerves! Adam lives in Arizona with his wife and their daughter.

Pack-n-Go Girls Online

Dying to know when the next Pack-n-Go Girls book will be out? Want to learn more German or how to yodel? Trying to figure out what to pack for your next trip? Looking for cool family travel tips? Interested in some fun learning activities about Austria to use at home or at school while you are reading *Mystery of the Ballerina Ghost*?

- Check out our website:
  www.packngogirls.com
- Follow us on Twitter:
  @packngogirls
- Like us on Facebook:
  facebook.com/packngogirls
- Follow us on Instagram:
  packngogirlsadventures
- Discover great ideas on Pinterest:
  Pack-n-Go Girls

63850927R00059

Made in the USA
Lexington, KY
19 May 2017